SAIL AWAY

The ballad of Skip and Nell

by **Mem Fox**
illustrated by **Pamela Lofts**

ASHTON SCHOLASTIC
SYDNEY AUCKLAND NEW YORK TORONTO LONDON

'Twas in the Northern Territory
Two dingo pups did dwell.
The cattlemen, their neighbours,
Called 'em Skip and Little Nell.

One night, beside a low camp fire,
They heard the men talk loud
About a boat-race way out west
That'd make all Aussies proud.

One said he'd give his two eye teeth
To be there at the race.
'My oath, too right!' the other said,
With longing on his face.

SAIL AWAY
The ballad of Skip and Nell

Sail Away

For Christo, Ferg and A.B.
And for Rory

National Library of Australia

Cataloguing-in-Publication data

Fox, Mem, 1946-
   Sail away! The ballad of Skip and Nell.

   ISBN 0 86896 360 7.
   ISBN 0 86896 355 0 (pbk.).

   1. Children's poetry, Australian. 2. Animals -
   Juvenile poetry. I. Lofts, Pamela. II. Title.
A821'.3

First published in 1986 by Ashton Scholastic Pty Limited (inc. in NSW),
PO Box 579, Gosford 2250. Also in Brisbane, Melbourne, Adelaide, Perth
and Auckland, NZ.

Typeset by Gardiner Initiates Pty Limited, Gosford NSW.

Printed in Hong Kong

6 5 4

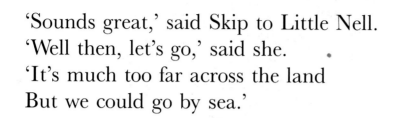

'Sounds great,' said Skip to Little Nell.
'Well then, let's go,' said she.
'It's much too far across the land
But we could go by sea.'

The dingo pair set out to sea –
Their hearts were beating fast.
Their boat was but a redgum log
With neither sail nor mast.

Before too long the log turned east
And Skip began to yell.
'We should be going west!' he cried.
'Tough luck,' said Little Nell.

'We'll get there in the end,' she said,
'It's just a longer trip.
We'll see that race, I promise you!'
'I hope you're right,' said Skip.

They travelled up and round and down
And then at last pulled in
To happy Queensland, Sunshine State,
To visit kith and kin.

They made a friend while they were there,
An old cane-toad called Clyde.
'I've heard about that race,' he said,
'Would you give me a ride?'

They hollowed out the log some more,
To give them extra space,
And once again they all set off
For that important race.

In New South Wales they stopped a while
To add a mast and sail.
'Now cheer up, Skip,' said Little Nell,
'With these we'll never fail.'

They took on board a cockatoo –
'Ah, let me come,' she'd cried.
So Skip and Nell and Clyde and bird
Sailed out upon the tide.

'It's hopeless, Little Nell,' said Skip.
'We're travelling much too slow.
We'll never get to Perth on time!
We'll miss the whole darn show.'

'Now Skip,' said Nell, 'enough of that.
Of course we'll get there, mate.
I'll just design a bigger boat
And THEN we won't be late.'

Their next stop was Victoria,
Where near the Yarra blue,
A wombat friend whose name was Ben,
Decided he'd come too.

They all began, as good mates will,
To work both night and day
Until that boat was re-designed –
'Three cheers! Hip, hip, hooray!'

They sailed towards Tasmania
Did Skip and Little Nell,
And Ben and Clyde and cockatoo
Felt sea-sick from the swell.

'Twas there a Tassie Devil rare,
Named Rupert, leapt aboard,
'I want to join your famous crew,
And see that race,' he roared.

'We'll need another sail,' said Nell.
'South Oz'll be the place
To buy a splendid spinnaker
To take us to the race.'

'Twas there they found the bright red sail
Which made their boat complete.
'Twas there they named it *Dinki Di*
And Nell's heart skipped a beat.

A kangaroo then joined the crew,
The one whose name was Kate.
'Well, hurry up and get on board,'
Said Skip, 'or we'll be late.'

Across the Bight, through massive seas
The *Dinki Di* was tossed,
By waves so high they reached the sky
And Skip thought all was lost.

And then at last the wind died down,
The *Dinki Di* stood still.
'We'll never make it now,' said Skip.
And even Nell felt ill.

But friendly dolphins passing by
Gave 'em a helpful shove;
They pushed that boat right on to Perth,
While Cocky flew above.

'Be quick! Be quick!' the cocky cried.
'The race has just begun!'
'Ah, stone the crows!' yelled Little Nell.
'I've never had such fun!'

The dolphins pushed with all their might –
The boat sped through the spray.
'WE'RE IN THE RACE!' cried Little Nell.
And Skip knelt down to pray.

They raced past boats both big and small,
They passed them, every one!
The crowd went mad and roared and cheered –
The *Dinki Di* had won!

Now that all happened long ago,
But I remember well
The day that boat-race, far out west
Was won by Skip and Nell.